ZOEYS GREAT ADVENTURE

ZOEYS GREAT ADVENTURE

BY CODY CONNOLLY

CONTENTS

CHAPTER 1

The Adventure Begins

ONCE UPON A TIME IN A CHARMING LITTLE TOWN, THERE LIVED A SPIRITED GIRL NAMED ZOEY. WITH HER WILD CURLS AND A PERPETUAL SPARKLE IN HER EYES, ZOEY WAS KNOWN FOR HER BOUNDLESS CURIOSITY AND ADVENTUROUS SPIRIT. ONE SUNNY DAY, AS ZOEY EXPLORED THE WOODS NEAR HER HOME, SHE STUMBLED UPON AN ANCIENT-LOOKING MAP TUCKED BENEATH A MOSS-COVERED ROCK. INTRIGUED, SHE DECIDED TO EMBARK ON A QUEST TO UNCOVER THE MYSTERY IT HELD. FOLLOWING THE MAP'S TWISTS AND TURNS, ZOEY JOURNEYED THROUGH ENCHANTED FORESTS AND CROSSED BABBLING BROOKS. ALONG THE WAY, SHE ENCOUNTERED TALKING ANIMALS AND FRIENDLY SPRITES WHO OFFERED GUIDANCE AND ENCOURAGEMENT.AS ZOEY VENTURED DEEPER INTO THE HEART OF THE FOREST, SHE DISCOVERED A HIDDEN GLADE ADORNED WITH SPARKLING CRYSTALS. IN THE CENTER STOOD A MAJESTIC TREE, ITS BRANCHES FORMING A NATURAL CANOPY. BENEATH IT LAY A TREASURE CHEST,

GUARDED BY WISE OLD OWLS. WITH A TWINKLE IN HER EYE, ZOEY UNLOCKED THE CHEST TO FIND NOT GOLD OR JEWELS, BUT A COLLECTION OF MAGICAL BOOKS. EACH BOOK CONTAINED STORIES OF FORGOTTEN LANDS AND MYTHICAL CREATURES. THE WISE OWLS EXPLAINED THAT ZOEY, WITH HER ADVENTUROUS SPIRIT, WAS CHOSEN TO BE THE GUARDIAN OF THESE TALES. FROM THAT DAY FORWARD, ZOEY BECAME THE STORYTELLER OF THE TOWN. EVERY WEEKEND, CHILDREN AND ADULTS ALIKE GATHERED IN THE ENCHANTED GLADE TO LISTEN TO HER MAGICAL TALES. THE ONCE-HIDDEN FOREST BECAME A PLACE OF WONDER AND JOY, ALL THANKS TO ZOEY'S INSATIABLE CURIOSITY AND THE MAGICAL STORIES

CHAPTER 2

Guardian of Dreams

IN THE SECOND CHAPTER OF ZOEY'S ADVENTURES, OUR SPIRITED HEROINE FOUND HERSELF DRAWN TO A MYSTERIOUS PORTAL THAT APPEARED IN THE HEART OF THE ENCHANTED FOREST. INTRIGUED AND FEARLESS AS EVER, ZOEY DECIDED TO STEP THROUGH THE SHIMMERING GATEWAY. ON THE OTHER SIDE, SHE DISCOVERED A MAGICAL REALM FILLED WITH FLOATING ISLANDS AND VIBRANT COLORS. THE AIR WAS FILLED WITH THE SWEET SCENT OF BLOOMING FLOWERS, AND FRIENDLY CREATURES WELCOMED HER WITH JOYOUS MELODIES. GUIDED BY A MISCHIEVOUS FAIRY, ZOEY EXPLORED THE FLOATING ISLANDS, EACH ONE PRESENTING A UNIQUE CHALLENGE OR PUZZLE. WITH HER CLEVER MIND AND ADVENTUROUS SPIRIT, SHE SOLVED RIDDLES, BEFRIENDED MAGICAL BEINGS, AND EVEN LEARNED TO RIDE ON THE BACKS OF SHIMMERING DRAGONFLIES.AT THE SUMMIT OF THE HIGHEST ISLAND, ZOEY ENCOUNTERED THE GUARDIAN OF DREAMS, A MAJESTIC CREATURE WITH FEATHERS THAT

SPARKLED LIKE STARDUST. THE GUARDIAN REVEALED THAT ZOEY'S ARRIVAL WAS FORETOLD IN THE ANCIENT SCROLLS, AND SHE WAS CHOSEN TO BRING BACK THE LOST DREAMS OF THE WORLD. WITH A WAVE OF THE GUARDIAN'S WING, ZOEY WAS SURROUNDED BY A SWIRL OF COLORFUL DREAMS. EACH DREAM REPRESENTED THE HOPES AND ASPIRATIONS OF THOSE WHO HAD FORGOTTEN HOW TO DREAM. ZOEY, WITH HER OPEN HEART, EMBRACED THESE DREAMS, VOWING TO SHARE THEM WITH THE WORLD. RETURNING THROUGH THE PORTAL, ZOEY BROUGHT THE MAGICAL DREAMS TO HER HOMETOWN. IN THE ENCHANTED GLADE, SHE SHARED THE DREAMS WITH THE EAGER LISTENERS. AS THE DREAMS TOUCHED THEIR HEARTS, THE TOWNSFOLK FELT A RENEWED SENSE OF WONDER AND INSPIRATION. AND SO, ZOEY'S SECOND CHAPTER UNFOLDED, REVEALING NOT ONLY HER COURAGE AND CURIOSITY BUT ALSO HER NEWFOUND ROLE AS THE KEEPER OF DREAMS. THE ENCHANTED FOREST BECAME A PLACE WHERE DREAMS CAME TO LIFE, ALL THANKS TO THE SPIRITED GIRL NAMED ZOEY. THE TOWNSPEOPLE, NOW FILLED WITH RENEWED HOPE, EAGERLY AWAITED THE NEXT CHAPTER OF HER ENCHANTING ADVENTURES.

CHAPTER 3

Time Traveling

IN THE THIRD CHAPTER OF ZOEY'S EXTRAORDINARY JOURNEY, THE ENCHANTED FOREST WHISPERED TALES OF A HIDDEN REALM BEHIND THE CASCADING WATERFALL. UNDETERRED BY THE MYSTERY, ZOEY, WITH HER ADVENTUROUS SPIRIT, SET OUT TO UNCOVER THE SECRETS THAT AWAITED HER. AS SHE APPROACHED THE ROARING WATERFALL, THE AIR BUZZED WITH ANTICIPATION. ZOEY DISCOVERED A HIDDEN PASSAGE BEHIND THE CURTAIN OF WATER, LEADING HER TO A LUMINOUS CAVERN ADORNED WITH GLOWING CRYSTALS. IN THE HEART OF THE CAVERN, SHE ENCOUNTERED THE GUARDIAN OF TIME. THE GUARDIAN, A WISE AND ANCIENT TORTOISE, EXPLAINED THAT ZOEY HAD BEEN CHOSEN TO SAFEGUARD THE BALANCE OF TIME. THE MAGICAL HOURGLASSES WITHIN THE CAVERN HELD THE THREADS OF PAST, PRESENT, AND FUTURE, AND ONLY ZOE COULD ENSURE THEIR HARMONIOUS FLOW. GUIDED BY THE GUARDIAN, ZOEY EMBARKED ON A JOURNEY THROUGH THE

CORRIDORS OF TIME. SHE WITNESSED HISTORICAL MOMENTS, FELT THE HEARTBEAT OF ANCIENT CIVILIZATIONS, AND GLIMPSED INTO THE DREAMS OF FUTURE GENERATIONS. ALONG THE WAY, SHE ENCOUNTERED FIGURES FROM THE PAST AND FUTURE, LEARNING VALUABLE LESSONS THAT TRANSCENDED THE BOUNDARIES OF TIME. IN THE PRESENT, ZOEY STOOD AT THE CENTER OF THE CAVERN, WHERE THE THREADS OF TIME CONVERGED. WITH A GENTLE TOUCH, SHE ENSURED THAT EACH GRAIN OF SAND FLOWED SEAMLESSLY THROUGH THE HOURGLASSES, MAINTAINING THE DELICATE BALANCE. AS ZOEY EMERGED FROM THE CAVERN, THE ENCHANTED FOREST SEEMED TO ECHO WITH THE WHISPERS OF GRATITUDE FROM THE PAST AND THE CHEERS OF HOPE FROM THE FUTURE. THE TOWNSPEOPLE, UNAWARE OF ZOEY'S TIME-TRAVELING ADVENTURES, FELT A SUBTLE SHIFT IN THE AIR—A RENEWED SENSE OF CONNECTION TO THE THREADS OF TIME THAT BOUND THEM ALL. AND SO, THE SPIRITED GIRL NAMED ZOEY, WITH HER COURAGE AND CURIOSITY, BECAME NOT ONLY THE GUARDIAN OF DREAMS BUT ALSO THE KEEPER OF TIME. THE ENCHANTED FOREST, NOW ENRICHED WITH THE MAGIC OF DREAMS AND THE HARMONY OF TIME, AWAITED THE UNFOLDING OF THE NEXT CHAPTER IN ZOEY'S EXTRAORDINARY TALE.

CHAPTER 4

Guardian of the Cosmos

IN THE FINAL CHAPTER OF ZOEY'S ENCHANTING JOURNEY, WHISPERS OF A CELESTIAL GATHERING REACHED HER EARS. THE STARS ALIGNED IN A DAZZLING DISPLAY, BECKONING ZOEY TO A CLEARING IN THE HEART OF THE ENCHANTED FOREST. THERE, BENEATH THE SHIMMERING NIGHT SKY, ZOEY DISCOVERED A COSMIC COUNCIL OF MYSTICAL BEINGS. THEY REVEALED THAT ZOEY'S ADVENTURES HAD WOVEN A TAPESTRY OF MAGIC, CONNECTING DREAMS, TIME, AND THE VERY ESSENCE OF THE UNIVERSE. THE CELESTIAL BEINGS BESTOWED UPON ZOEY A LUMINOUS AMULET, SYMBOLIZING HER ROLE AS THE GUARDIAN OF THE COSMOS. WITH THIS AMULET, ZOEY COULD CHANNEL THE ENERGY OF THE STARS TO BRING HARMONY AND WONDER TO THE WORLD. AS ZOEY EMBRACED HER COSMIC DESTINY, A RADIANT GLOW SURROUNDED HER, ILLUMINATING THE ENTIRE FOREST. THE TOWNSPEOPLE, DRAWN BY THE ETHEREAL LIGHT, GATHERED IN THE ENCHANTED GLADE. ZOEY, NOW ADORNED WITH THE AMULET,

SHARED STORIES THAT TRANSCENDED THE BOUNDARIES OF IMAGINATION, INTERTWINING DREAMS, TIME, AND THE COSMIC TAPESTRY. THE ENCHANTED FOREST, ONCE A HIDDEN REALM, BECAME A BEACON OF INSPIRATION FOR ALL WHO VENTURED WITHIN. ZOEY'S TALES ECHOED IN THE HEARTS OF THE TOWNSPEOPLE, CREATING A LEGACY OF WONDER AND UNITY. WITH A TWINKLE IN HER EYE AND THE COSMIC AMULET GLEAMING, ZOEY CONTINUED TO SHARE STORIES, ENSURING THAT THE MAGIC OF DREAMS, THE HARMONY OF TIME, AND THE COSMIC WONDERS WOULD ENDURE FOR GENERATIONS TO COME. AND SO, THE SPIRITED GIRL NAMED ZOEY, WITH HER BOUNDLESS COURAGE AND INSATIABLE CURIOSITY, BECAME A TIMELESS LEGEND, FOREVER REMEMBERED AS THE GUARDIAN OF DREAMS, THE KEEPER OF TIME, AND THE COSMIC WEAVER OF ENCHANTMENT. AS THE ENCHANTED FOREST ECHOED WITH LAUGHTER AND DREAMS, ZOEY'S STORY BECAME AN EVERLASTING SOURCE OF INSPIRATION AND MAGIC IN THE HEARTS OF ALL WHO LISTENED, ZOEY RETURNED HOME, NOT ONLY WITH CHERISHED MEMORIES OF HER GREAT ADVENTURE BUT ALSO WITH A NEWFOUND UNDERSTANDING OF THE MAGIC THAT EXISTS IN THE EVERYDAY MOMENTS OF LIFE. AND SO, ZOEY'S GREAT ADVENTURE BECAME A STORY WHISPERED. UNTILL NEXT TIME.

THE END

Dear Readers, As I pen down these words, my heart is filled with gratitude and warmth. I want to express my sincerest thanks to each one of you who embarked on the journey through the pages of my book, Your support and enthusiasm have been the driving force behind this creative endeavor. It's a humbling experience to know that my words have found a place in your minds and hearts. Your feedback and encouragement have been a source of inspiration, pushing me to explore new depths and craft stories that resonate with you. Every reader is a co-traveler on the adventure within the book's universe, and I am genuinely thankful for the time you've invested in exploring the realms I've created. Your connection with the characters and the narrative is what makes storytelling truly magical. Whether you found solace in the words during challenging times or simply enjoyed the escapism, your engagement with the book has given it life beyond the written pages. Please accept my heartfelt thanks for being a part of this literary journey. Your support is a treasure that I will forever cherish. With sincere gratitude.

To Zoey Love Dad

www.ingramcontent.com/pod-product-compliance
Lightning Source LLC
Chambersburg PA
CBHW061225210726

48294CB00006B/1984